Lucien's Mate
Soul Mates
Book 1

Diana Persaud

Copyright © 2014 Diana Persaud

All rights reserved.

ISBN:150539435X
ISBN-13: 978-1505394351

DEDICATION

To my Darling Sugar Drawers,

Thank You for your faith in me.

-Your one and only Pumpkin Head

CHAPTER ONE

The door opened and he suddenly forgot how to breathe. Sights and sounds around him disappeared as he focused on *her*. He watched her while she spoke to the waitress, ran her hand through her short black hair. His eyes never left her as she walked across the room to the bar at the back of the restaurant. Her hips swayed slightly and he admired the way her jeans hugged her round ass. He wondered how good it would feel to hold her hips while he rubbed his cock against her generous bottom. His cock began to twitch in anticipation. His pack mates stared at him in shocked silence as he got up and walked across the room to the bar.

Lanie hurried into Jack's, a local restaurant that catered exclusively to werewolves. She opened the door and stepped into the quaint restaurant. Laughter and loud voices greeted her as well as the scent of delicious Italian food. Behind the hostess podium, she noted an almost full restaurant. Diners sat at the tables enjoying red wine and pasta. Pasta was their specialty and their garlic bread was to die for! She was certain Heaven had an unlimited supply of Jack's garlic bread.

It was fairly early for the dinner crowd and she was surprised to see so many patrons here. This was her last errand today and she was anxious to get back to her darling triplets. Tessa greeted her warmly and informed her that they were unusually busy today, so they were a little behind on her daily order. At Tessa's suggestion, she decided to wait in the bar.

"What'll it be, darlin'?" Toby asked as he wiped down the counter. Lanie yawned as she sat down.

"Just coffee. I'm so tired I could fall asleep standing up!" She stifled another yawn, arched her back and stretched her arms behind her head, unaware the action pushed her breasts outward.

Toby licked his lips as he stared at her breasts and swore he heard a growl. His eyes snapped up and he saw the pissed off man behind her. He paled as recognition set in.

"Toby? What's wrong? You look...." Scared as hell, she thought. What could possibly scare the tough looking bartender, she wondered as she turned around. She sucked in a breath, shocked at the man standing right behind her. Lanie could swear she heard warning bells going off in her head. The man exuded danger.

At six feet tall, he towered over her. He had short, thick black hair and the most beautiful blue eyes she had ever seen. His goatee only accentuated the three long scars across his right cheek. He looked seriously pissed at Toby. He clenched his jaw and she saw the muscle there jump. His shirt clung to his massive chest and flat belly. He also had muscular arms, something she definitely appreciated. His fists were clenched at his sides. His entire body was tense, as if ready for a fight. She heard Toby swear and back away. She thought she heard him say, "Shit man, I didn't know…."

The stranger's eyes followed Toby as he moved away. Once Toby was out of his sight, he relaxed his stance, tension completely gone. He moved to sit on the barstool next to her and turned to face her. He leaned slightly toward her, closed his eyes and inhaled her scent. His eyes snapped open and he looked at her, confusion on his face. She smelled of baby powder and had the unmistakable scent of pups, yet he could smell no man's scent on her body. He was about to say something when Lanie's cell phone rang.

She glanced at the caller ID and saw it was her brother, Michael. She answered and listened for a minute.

"ALL of them?! Shit, don't they have any damn manners?...Ok, Ok, I'll get some more food, but they are busy here so it may take a while. I'm at Jack's now, waiting for our usual order… mmmhmmm. How are the kids? …Oh, good. All right, I'll see you in a bit…bye."

As she hung up, Tessa walked up and told her the food was almost ready.

"I hate to do this to you, but Taylor and the rest of his brothers just showed up, so we'll need at least another lasagna…and a bunch of bread sticks."

"Better make it TWO lasagnas and extra breadsticks. I know how those boys eat. I'll put a rush on it. I know you are anxious to get back to the girls, Lanie," Tessa said with a smile as she walked away.

Lanie smiled as she thought of her little nieces, barely two weeks old.

"He's a worthless bastard to get you with pups then abandon you. You deserve better than that. *I* will provide for you and your pups. And in time, we will have our own."

"Excuse me?" A very shocked Lanie turned to the man sitting beside her.

"Ahh…umm…." She floundered for something else to say. *Just what in the hell was he suggesting?*

She was about to ask him when she heard someone call her name. She turned to the door and saw Riley walking towards her.

Hot damn, the man was good looking. Her body reacted at the mere sight of him.

He could smell her sudden arousal and it angered him that *he* wasn't the cause. He looked at the tall blond man striding towards them. Realization hit him.

"It's him, isn't it? I'll kill the worthless bastard," she heard him growl as he stood up.

"Wait! You have it all wrong," Lanie called out as she raced after him. She tried to grab his shirt, but he moved too damn fast. She did the only thing she could think of. She shoved him and he fell into a group of patrons. She quickly moved around him, to step in front of Riley. She put her hand on Riley's chest to stop him. Lanie heard a loud, menacing growl. She turned around and held up her hand at the advancing stranger. He looked ready to tear Riley apart.

"He didn't do anything…he's not the father, my brother is!" She said. When she saw the shock on his face, she quickly clarified.

"What I meant was, my brother and his *wife* had triplets. I'm just here helping out." That seemed to calm him down tremendously. She shook her head and let out a long breath, relieved that Riley hadn't been hurt. *This man had been ready to fight over* her?

"What are you doing here, Riley? I thought you and your brothers were at Mike's?"

"Mike said you came to pick up food and I thought you might need a hand," Riley replied.

Just then, Tessa walked up with two heavy bags, announcing their order was ready. Lanie asked Riley to take the food home and assured him she would be right behind him. She turned to the stranger behind her and sighed.

"I…ah… think it was very sweet of you to…umm… your offer was….ahh….it's obviously not necessary, so bye!" She turned and practically ran out the door.

He frowned slightly at her flight. At least he knew her name. *Lanie*. He walked over to the waitress, Tessa, determined to find out everything about *his* Lanie.

Later that night….

Her youngest niece finally fell asleep. After gently placing her into her bassinet, Lanie went to bed. She replayed the day's events and thought she must have been in a twilight zone episode. *There was no way any man, especially such an attractive one, would ever offer to take care of* me. *Especially if he thought I had someone else's kid. But this guy did offer. Didn't he? Maybe I misunderstood. Didn't he say something about having kids with me? This is so confusing. Didn't most men run at the mere thought of marriage and a family? This one obviously didn't.*

There must be something wrong with him, she concluded. She turned to her side, still thinking about the blue eyed stranger from the bar.

Maybe his vision is going. After all, I'm hardly what anyone would call attractive.

At a little over five feet tall, she had short brown hair, plain brown eyes and excess weight.

My breasts are too small, my hips and butt are too big. Men like him prefer tall, leggy, voluptuous blonds, everything I'm not. Wait a minute. I know what's wrong with him. He must be a werewolf! She sighed. *It figures that the only guy to ever* show *interest in me was part wolf. That makes him off limits then. There was no way a wolf pack would ever accept a human.*

She thought back to the day she found out about werewolves, almost two weeks ago....

It was finally happening! Her sister in law, Devon, was going to have her babies. She wasn't sure why Devon insisted on having her babies at home. She was expecting triplets, which was why Lanie decided to spend her summer vacation with her brother, Michael, and his wife. She knew they would need an extra hand to deal with three screaming babies.

Hell, IF I ever have a kid, I want an Epidural. Shit! Maybe two or three, thought Lanie, as she heard her sister-in-law scream in pain. Several minutes later, she heard the distinct cry of a baby, then another cry and at last, one more. Three healthy baby girls were born.

Several hours later, she heard a loud sound coming from the nursery. She jumped out of her chair and ran to the room. Her heart stopped beating as she stared at the empty bassinet. She screamed and heard her brother come running into the room. A movement on the floor caught her eye. It was a wolf pup.

"Oh, My God! It killed the baby!" she screamed and reached for the lamp. She was going to throw it at the wolf pup when her brother snatched it out of her hands. He dropped the lamp and grabbed her by her arms.

"Listen to me! The baby is fine. The baby is safe!" he said as he shook her. Finally she calmed down.

"Safe? Nellie is safe? Where is she? Where's Nellie? No one came in here…."

Her brother swore and then said, "The wolf pup… is Nellie."

Lanie stared at him in disbelief. He explained how several years ago he had been attacked by a werewolf. Most people who were attacked usually died. The few who survived a werewolf attack always became werewolves. No one knew why. A werewolf leader, called an Alpha, heard about his attack and brought him here, to Second Chances, where he could live safely among others of his kind. It was here that he met and fell in love with his mate, Devon. About half of the citizens of Second Chances were werewolves.

"Usually pups don't change this young unless they are frightened." Michael said worriedly.

"I heard a sound. Maybe it scared her and she changed…into…a…wolf." She still couldn't believe it. But she did believe when she saw the wolf pup, which had just fallen asleep cradled in her brother's arms, change back into her oldest niece.

Lanie, a science teacher, now believed in werewolves. Why hadn't they been discovered yet? Then she remembered how her brother had sworn her to secrecy. What else was out there? Vampires? Leprechauns? Bigfoot?! She had a million questions for her brother and sister in law, but they became so busy with the triplets, she never got a chance to ask any of them.

She sighed yet again. One of these days she would find out if she needed to stock up on silver bullets, holy water and garlic. She fell asleep and dreamed of a large black wolf with familiar blue eyes.

CHAPTER TWO

This can't be happening, thought Lanie as she glanced around Jake's. It was packed…with pack. She was surrounded by werewolves. Members from neighboring packs had sent representatives to Second Chances to celebrate the birth of her triplet nieces.

I bet he *is here. What if he* says *something?* She was still embarrassed about running away from him like a scared virgin, but she wasn't sure what to do when a man looked at her with such intensity. Not once in her twenty five years had a man ever looked at her the way *he* did. Then there was the small issue of the warning bells she heard.

What was that all about anyway? She panicked at another thought. *What if he ignored her? Or worse, what if he was here with another woman? Shit! It's best to just avoid him altogether.* Especially since for the last three nights, she did nothing but dream of a large black wolf with his blue eyes.

He stood across the room and watched her. She looked lovely in her yellow floral dress. It clung to her in all the right places. He absently wondered what she wore underneath. His cock began to twitch and harden as he contemplated her underwear. Sexy lace panties? A thong? He swore he would buy her crotch less panties so he could just bend her over and take her without removing a stitch of clothing. His cock throbbed at the thought of entering her.

When she picked up the crying baby and soothed it, both his heart and loins clenched tightly. He wanted her. He wanted her holding *his* child. Holding *their* child. He had never considered having kids before. But then again, he had never contemplated settling down, either.

Not until he saw *her*.

Lanie caught a whiff and knew it was time for a diaper change. She turned around and disappeared though a door behind her. The small office had been set up as a temporary nursery for her three nieces. A microwave had been placed on the oak desk and the small refrigerator stocked with milk instead of beer. Three empty bassinettes stood in front of the oak desk. She changed and fed Jules. Not wanting to go back outside and risk seeing him, she decided to rock Jules. Within minutes, her tiny niece was asleep. She gently laid her in the bassinet and watched her sleep. Feeling guilty about leaving Devon with the other two babies, she worked up the courage to go back outside. Nellie needed a change, so she took her back inside.

He watched her as she took the last child into the room and wondered how long she would stay in there this time. He knew they would never allow him into the room, so he would have to wait until she got hungry. He would get his chance then. He smiled and settled into his chair, fantasizing about all the ways he could and *would* fuck her.

Lanie was starving. She'd only eaten half her lunch when the girls woke up and she never had a chance to finish it. Now her belly was growling rather loudly. She bit her bottom lip and decided to take a chance. *He's probably already left. After all, who in their right mind wants to stay and look at three kids that aren't even theirs? Besides me, I mean.* With that thought, she bravely opened the door and snuck out.

Because his eyes never left the door, he saw when she opened it and quietly snuck out. She kept her head down and was trying very hard not to make eye contact with anyone. She headed directly for the buffet. *BINGO!* He reached the buffet when she did and reached for the plate at the same time.

"Sorry," Lanie said, without looking up.

"You can make it up to me," he said. She heard his deep voice and looked up. Her eyes widened and she sucked in a breath.

He took two plates, handing her one. He filled both of their plates, gently guiding her along with his hand on her elbow. Lanie was still shocked speechless. He wore a blue cotton shirt that accentuated his eyes, wide chest and his muscular arms. *He was here! He is talking to* me. *And I have no idea what to say to him.*

"Lucien! You are the only Alpha to honor us by attending this celebration. Come, sit with me," requested Ethan, the Alpha of the Second Chances pack. Lucien turned to Lanie.

"Shall we?" he asked.

She stared at him with wide eyes and shook her head. *Have dinner with two Alphas? I couldn't handle one Alpha, much less two.*

Lucien turned to Ethan and declined with a smile, "I would be honored to dine with you, Ethan, but Lanie is much easier on the eyes than you are." Ethan laughed and nodded in understanding.

"Even my mate would agree with you. Enjoy your dinner."

His name was Lucien and he wants to dine with me. She was both elated and terrified at the same time. He guided her to an intimate table for two.

I'm more important than making nice with another Alpha? She wasn't sure that was such a good idea. She didn't know much about werewolf politics, but politics was politics.

"Um….are you sure that was wise? Turning him down, I mean." Lucien raised an eyebrow.

"Are you questioning my decision as an Alpha?" *Shit. Not even two minutes in his company and already I offended him.*

"I just meant that….um…you know…politics?" *Why can't I form a coherent sentence when he is around?*

"You're absolutely right. I came here to celebrate the birth of your nieces as well as for… political reasons," Lucien amended. "But then I met you, and you are far more important than pack politics." She saw the way he looked at her and her body responded. She felt a sudden tightness in her belly. He scented her arousal and smiled, knowing *he* was the cause.

"Um.…"

"Are you going to run away again?" Lucien asked softly. "My wolf loves the thrill of a chase."

"Are…are you talking about…is this a separate wolf…or…a.…"

"My wolf and I are one and the same. Sometimes I

am more like a man in terms of thinking, and other times, I am more like a wolf, in both thoughts and actions."

"So…what are you most like now?" Lanie asked, genuinely curious.

Lucien leaned close. "The man wants to seduce you with words. The wolf wants to throw you over my shoulder, take you to my bed and pleasure you until you say you are *mine*."

"Oh?"

Lucien leaned in closer and spoke in a soft, seductive voice. "My wolf is impatient and curious. I'm dying to know Lanie, lace panties, thong or nothing at all?"

"What?" *This is a highly inappropriate conversation. I should put a stop to it.*

"Or perhaps you would like me to check?" He leaned in, placed a hand on her knee and Lanie shook her head.

"White cotton."

What is wrong with me? This man is beyond rude, inquiring about my underwear and I'm describing it to him! Only to stop him from checking, she told herself.

"My wolf is pleased. Do you want to know what my wolf would do to you, Lanie?" Not really, she thought as she nodded. *Why is my body not listening to my head?*

"He would have me rip off your dress and your panties, so that I could suck on your nipples. I would push you onto my bed, spread your legs wide so I could lick your sweet spot. Would you spread your legs for me, Lanie? Hold them open while I lick you?"

Though she was speechless, her body reacted to his words. She was surprised at the sudden sharp stab of 'pain' she felt in her middle. Only the sensation wasn't painful, it was intense. *Was this desire? Did my womb contract?* She became wet, felt an unfamiliar ache begin to form between her legs.

"I'm dying to taste you, to bury my tongue deep inside of you. I could spend hours tasting you, fucking you with just my tongue. Then I would use my fingers. Would you like to feel my fingers inside of you? Or would you prefer that I spread your legs and fuck you until you screamed my name and begged me to take you again?"

"Jesus," Lanie said as she felt her womb tighten more as flashes of pleasure/pain ran through her body. Lanie felt a sudden flood of wetness between her legs. Her mouth went dry and she licked her lips.

"Lanie…," he said in a gruff voice. Desire darkened his eyes and his erection throbbed painfully. His hand moved up her thigh, pushing her dress up.

The way he said her name made her even more aroused. Her womb clenched and unclenched. *Am I having an orgasm? With* just *his words?* Then what would he do with his body, she wondered.

Lucien could smell how aroused she had become. Saw the way her breathing changed, the way she bit her bottom lip, the way her brown eyes dilated. It took everything in his power not to hoist her over his shoulder and carry her off to his bed, cave man style.

"You don't play fair, do you?"

"I'm not playing, Lanie. I want you and you want me too. I can see the desire in your eyes. Give me a chance to win you, Lanie. I will cherish and protect you. I will satisfy you as no other could."

Geez, was this guy a mind reader? She was going to melt into a puddle if he didn't stop. *It has to be bullshit. No way does he mean it. Why does he have to look so good and smell so divine? And say all the right things… how am I ever going to say no?* Suddenly, she remembered the warning bells that rang in her head when she first met him. She sat up straight and decided she would run. *Wolf be damned. I can't handle a man like this. He was just too…intense.*

"The girls! I…I better go check on them." She got up and practically ran into their room. Lucien watched her go. His wolf was pleased. Let the chase begin.…

CHAPTER THREE

The next day, Lanie stared at the dozen red roses in his hand. She was stunned.

"For me? No one's ever given me flowers before...."

The roses were blood red and had a light sweet scent. Lanie closed her eyes and inhaled, delighted at the scent. She took the roses to the kitchen and placed them in a vase. She turned and smiled at him.

"Thank you, they are lovely."

"So are you."

She swallowed. *He thinks I'm lovely? How am I going to resist Lucien? Where the hell were those warning bells, anyway? Maybe I didn't really hear them. After all, that day I was so sleep deprived.... And last night at the restaurant? I'm sure I read more into his seductive words than he intended. Surely he didn't really mean he would do those things to* me*?*

"My mother is looking for a house. I found one a couple of hours away. I was wondering if you would like to check it out with me. I could really use a woman's perspective. Will you help me, Lanie?" How could she resist? He obviously needed her help, so she agreed. It's not like it was a date or anything, she reminded herself.

Lanie sat next to him in his pickup truck and he smiled contentedly as he drove towards his home town of Last Hope. So far, it had been a pleasant ride. He learned that she was a science teacher so she had the entire summer off. Luckily for Devon, she was due shortly after school ended, so Lanie was able to be there to help. Her love for her nieces was evident.

Lucien told her about how another pack, the Lost Souls, had threatened his pack when their Alpha became sick. The elders had reached out to him, convinced him to come back and fight to keep his pack and his family safe. He fought and killed several Lost Souls wolves in the battle to protect his pack. When the fight was over, the Lost Souls pack had retreated in fear of him. He had been named Alpha, the leader of Lost Hope two years ago.

"Is that how you got your scars?"

"Yes. Do they repulse you?" He tensed as he awaited her answer.

"Not at all."

She thought his scars were sexy. Hell, everything about him was attractive. She thought about running her fingers through his thick hair and tracing the scars on his face. She looked at his biceps, aching to touch them, squeeze them. She wondered how it would feel if he wrapped his arms around her. Her nipples hardened and she shook her head to clear her thoughts.

Lucien smiled when the distinct aroma of her arousal hit his nose. She wanted him, despite his scars. Most people flinched and looked away in fear when they saw him, even when he wasn't angry. Even female wolves avoided him after his battle with the Lost Souls. He had been brutal. He had to be. Lanie didn't fear him the way others did. She had only run away from him because he had been too blatant in his desire for her. He had let his wolf take the lead and it scared her. He planned on being much more subtle, allowing the man to seduce her.

He pulled the truck into the driveway. The real estate agent came out to greet them, and gave them a tour of the house. It was a lovely five bedroom house, complete with pool. It was situated on 3 acres of land, most of which was part of the forest. There was plenty of wild area for his wolf to run.

It had a large open floor plan with many updated amenities. As they walked through the house, Lanie commented on all the things she liked. She seemed especially fond of the large stone fireplace in the living room. The living room was already furnished with comfortable sofas and chairs. She sat in one and noted the kitchen beyond.

"Wow! This is the most amazing kitchen I have ever seen. Talk about Gourmet! A gas stove. And double ovens. I would kill to have a kitchen like this… Did you see the herb garden outside? I've always wanted an herb garden…." Lanie opened the door and went outside, identifying most of the herbs.

"Your wife seems taken with this house. There's plenty of room for you and any future children you might have." Mrs. Raymond smiled. Lanie heard what she said and blushed.

"It's not for us… I mean, it's for his mother." Mrs. Raymond turned to him with a puzzled expression on her face.

"But I thought you said—"

"Lanie, what do you think? Would you like living here?" She thought about it for a minute and said, "It's a bit large for just your mom and step dad, but the extra guest rooms will come in handy for when you and your brothers visit. I'm sure she'll love it. I do!"

"Then we'll take it."

He drove her into town for a late lunch. Billy Rae's Bar and Grill was the local pack meeting place. Like most restaurants, Billy Rae's had booths along the glass at the front, tables and chairs in the middle, making it easy to reconfigure during pack meetings and gatherings. The bar lined the wall along the back of the restaurant and next to it stood a raised dance floor. Next to the dance floor was a hallway that led to the bathrooms. It was early in the afternoon, so the restaurant was fairly empty. A few men sat on the bar stools at the bar. Lucien guided them to a table and Lanie excused herself, heading to the bathroom near the dance floor. Lucien greeted his two pack members at the bar and then headed to the bathroom as well.

When Lanie came out of the bathroom, she noticed three young men gathered around a young woman, pressed against the wall in the hallway. "Please stop it…Don't touch me!"

"Leave her alone," Lanie demanded. They turned and looked at her. Lanie pushed past them and grabbed the young woman's hand. She looked relieved. Lanie pulled her away from the wall and they began walking back toward the table. One of the men grabbed Lanie's arm, pulling her to a stop.

"Get your hand off me!" Lanie demanded as she

tried to pull away from him.

"I'm going to teach you to mind your own business, Cunt!" His friends moved to either side of her, holding her arms so she couldn't move. He pulled out a knife and moved towards her.

Lanie was livid. She kicked him as hard as she could in the crotch and when he doubled over in pain, she kneed him in the face. He fell down, grabbing his groin, bleeding from where she hit his nose. His friends released her and moved toward the young man on the floor.

"Holy Fuck! She kicked your ass! A human!" They laughed as they taunted him.

Lucien came out of the bathroom and his heart stopped when he saw Lanie being held by two young men. His shock quickly wore off and rage filled him. Lanie looked up in relief when she saw Lucien behind the young men. She was shocked at the look of pure rage on his face. The two men who were standing turned around, their laughter dying immediately when they saw Lucien.

"Did they hurt you, Lanie?" She moved past the men to touch him on the chest and he slipped his hands around her waist.

"I'm fine, Lucien. Really." Her touch and her words seemed to calm him considerably.

"Why are you in my territory?" he growled at the three men.

"Www...we were just looking for some tail."

"Some tail?" Lanie said angrily. She turned, about to walk over to them, but Lucien held her tightly around her waist, pulling her towards him.

"I don't know how you treat your females in the Lost Souls pack, but here, we treat them with respect.

To attack a female is to court death. You are lucky she is unharmed." All three gulped and paled even further. Lucien wanted nothing more than to kill them slowly for touching *his* Lanie. He feared she would despise his brutal nature. Not wanting to scare her away, he decided to spare the young men.

"Get out of my territory. If *any* of your pack dares to come here again, without my permission, they do so at the risk of death." They couldn't get out of Rae's fast enough.

He turned Lanie and pulled her into his arms, holding her tightly. After a few minutes, he released her enough to look at her eyes. "Promise me you will never put yourself at risk again."

"Lucien—"

"Promise me, Lanie! You could have been seriously hurt or even killed." Knowing he only worried about her safety, she conceded, "I won't go looking for any fights, but I'm not going to stand around and do nothing while they—"

"Next time, get reinforcements, then you can come back and kick their asses." Lanie nodded in agreement as she laughed and he joined her. The pack members at the bar stared in shock. Their Alpha was *laughing*.

Back at the table, Lucien listened as Anya and Lanie explained and couldn't fault her for intervening. He didn't notice his pack members busily texting on their cell phones.

"What are you doing here, Anya? Shouldn't you be in school? And why didn't you call for help?" Anya hung her head in shame.

"I'm sorry, Alpha. I cut class. I didn't want to draw attention because then my parents would know I cut class."

"Why? Isn't it summer time? Why are you in school?" asked Lanie. Anya looked at Lucien, who nodded.

"We have school year round. It keeps us out of trouble… I cut class because I hate sewing!"

"Sewing? Why did you take it then? Graduation requirements or are you stuck in a rotation?"

"They make us take it, so that when our mates get into fights, we can fix their ripped clothing."

"WHAT?" Lanie turned to Lucien, eyes flashing angrily. He held up both hands in an attempt to pacify her.

"Now wait a minute, I had no idea they were required to do this. It must have been something the previous Alpha required. He was a bit old fashioned. Let me guess, men should take sewing as well, so they can fix their own shirts?" She nodded.

"I'll make sure we change that immediately." Her smile was rewarding. He wondered what other outdated pack practices were still in place. He would have to assign someone to look into that. He smiled when he realized it would be the perfect project for his mate. It would be a good way for her to learn about his pack.

"I understand why you hate sewing class, but think of the benefits. You can make things for yourself. My aunts are avid sewers and they can make just about anything. I envy them those skills. If you really hate it that much, you can always switch classes. But you should check with your guidance counselor and make sure you are meeting all of your graduation requirements."

"Thanks. I'll think about it. I guess I should be

heading back to class."

"Next time, if you are in trouble, call for help. Getting into trouble with your parents is nothing compared to what could have happened." Anya nodded in agreement. Although she had been dismissed, Anya hesitated. Lanie didn't know much about wolves but she knew how she would feel. She turned to Lucien.

"Lucien, there might be more of those idiots out there. I would feel much better if someone took Anya back to school." Lucien agreed and noted that Anya visibly relaxed.

Lucien turned to the bar and called out to a one of his pack members. "Harley, can you take Anya back to school?" Harley nodded from his bar stool. He stood up and walked over to the table.

"Ever been on a bike before, kid?" When Anya shook her head, he said, "Then you're in for a real treat, let's go." Anya turned to leave, then on impulse turned around and hugged Lanie. Lanie hugged her tightly and Anya left with a smile on her face. Her belly rumbled and Lanie blushed with embarrassment. *Why does this always happen to me?*

"It's late and I'm famished," Lucien said with an amused smile.

"What's their specialty?"

"They make the best Philly Cheese Steak in the state."

"Then that's what I'll have."

As they enjoyed their lunch, more and more pack members came in. They laughed and teased each other throughout lunch, neither one noticing that pack members stared at them openly and exchanged knowing smiles.

Word had spread like wildfire. The Alpha had a *woman* at Rae's. One that made him smile and laugh. One he touched at every opportunity. Everyone wanted to see the woman who had kicked some major ass, saving the life of a young woman. As the story was passed on, more details were added and the story was embellished. By the end of the day, everyone was talking about how the Alpha's woman had singlehandedly taken on ten Lost Souls pack members, beaten them bloody and saved four young women from being viciously raped. The Lost Souls pack had pleaded for mercy before she finally let them go, tails between their legs. They were *honored* to have such a brave woman at their Alpha's side.

By the time they finished their lunch, Rae's was packed. Lucien wasn't surprised at all to see his pack members. He knew they were curious about his Lanie but no one wanted to interrupt his date. He planned on giving her a tour of their town before he convinced her to have dinner with him. Unfortunately, one of the triplets was sick and she had to return home.

On the drive back, he filled her in on some of his duties. He was essentially Judge, Jury and Executioner. He was charged with physically protecting his pack. He had a team of soldiers that helped him keep his town secure. He also ensured they were economically stable. He was sort of like the President and Congress rolled into one, while the elders were similar to the Supreme Court justices. He had many responsibilities to his pack and was available to them at all times.

"Except when I'm with you. You will always come first, Lanie." She had been so touched, she had allowed him to hold her and kiss her good bye. He leaned in and kissed her softly. Her arms slid up his shoulders as he pulled her close. He broke off the kiss to nibble on her neck and she groaned and held him tighter. Lucien couldn't resist sucking on a spot on her neck, marking her. His wolf grinned with satisfaction as he staked his claim. Lanie had no idea her neck was so sensitive or that his mouth on her neck would be so enjoyable. She rubbed against him, felt his erection and heat pooled between her legs. The door opened behind her and her brother stared at them in shock. Reluctantly, she pulled away and went inside after promising she would see him the next day.

CHAPTER FOUR

Lanie opened the door, surprised to see Lucien standing there. Lucien held up a picnic basket, smiling happily.

"I thought you might want lunch." Lanie smiled and nodded, opening the door so he could enter. Lucien walked in, paused in front of Lanie, slipped his arm around her waist and pulled her close to him. He lowered his head and kissed her. Lanie slid her arms up his chest and one hand slipped around his neck, pulling him closer. Lanie's body responded instantly to Lucien's kiss. Her nipples pebbled and her channel tightened. Nellie's cries interrupted their kiss and Lucien reluctantly released her.

Lanie closed the door and he followed her into the living room. Lanie went into the nursery to get Nellie while Lucien began arranging their picnic in the living room. He moved the coffee table, spread out a picnic blanket and began emptying the basket.

Lanie changed Nellie and brought her into the living room. She was astonished to find a picnic in her brother's living room.

"I need to make her bottle. Can you hold her for a minute?" Lucien nodded and she showed him how to position his arm to cradle the baby. She gently placed Nellie in the crook of his arm and her heart squeezed at the sight of Lucien holding her tiny niece. Lanie quickly made the bottle for her hungry niece and returned to the living room.

Lucien motioned for her to sit on the floor and she did. He returned the baby to her and she fed Nellie. Lucien went into the kitchen to wash his hands. When he returned, he sat next to Lanie and removed some containers from the picnic basket. He made a plate of fried chicken, potato salad and corn on the cob. He took out a fork, picked up some potato salad and held the fork in front of Lanie's mouth. She opened her mouth and he gently slipped it in.

"Chicken?" he asked and she nodded. Lucien picked up the drumstick and held it to her. Lanie took a bite and Lucien smiled with contentment. His wolf was pleased, satisfied with his ability to feed its mate. Lucien continued to feed Lanie, occasionally leaning over to lick potato salad from the side of her mouth then placing light kisses on her lips.

Once Nellie finished her bottle, Lanie burped her and soon after, she fell asleep. Lanie gently placed her on the blanket and moved closer to Lucien. He refused to let her feed herself, so she fixed him a plate and they fed each other. During their meal, she filled him in on the previous night's events. The three of them had been up all night with Jules and Bella. The girls kept crying and none of them had gotten much sleep. Mike and Devon had taken the two sick girls to the hospital early that morning. She yawned suddenly and Lucien noticed how tired she looked.

"Let's clean up this mess and you can take a nap with Nellie." Lanie gave him a grateful smile and they cleaned up.

Lucien tossed a pillow onto the floor so she could lie on her stomach next to Nellie. He straddled her and began massaging her shoulders. Lucien's strong hands on her shoulders and back was soothing. Within minutes, Lanie was fast asleep. His wolf growled low in satisfaction. His wolf enjoyed caring for its mate.

Nellie began fussing. Not wanting to wake Lanie, Lucien picked her up. He sat on the couch and growled low. The pup recognized him as an Alpha and whimpered softly. Lucien lay back on the couch with Nellie on his chest. He continued growling in a low, soothing tone as he stroked her back gently. Nellie burped loudly then fell asleep.

Sometime later, Lanie woke up from her nap and panicked when she noticed Nellie wasn't on the blanket next to her. She sat up and turned to the couch. Lanie's heart melted at the sight of Lucien, asleep on the couch with Nellie on his chest. She realized at that moment that she had fallen in love with Lucien.

Lanie sat there for a long time watching Lucien sleep. Could *they have a relationship? Lucien was an Alpha* werewolf *and she was a* human. Her heart filled with joy when she realized Lucien must think a relationship was possible, or he wouldn't be here, babysitting her niece while she rested.

The front door opened quietly and Lucien woke up. Mike and Devon entered, each carrying a baby carrier containing a sleeping child. Both looked exhausted and they were surprised to see Lucien in their home, with their daughter asleep on his chest. Neither one said anything, but the shock was evident on their faces.

"Well? What did the doctor say?" Lanie asked her brother.

"Stomach flu. They need lots of fluids and rest. They should be fine in a few days."

"Thank goodness! I was really worried. Let me take care of them while you two take a nap. I just woke up and I feel refreshed."

Grateful for the reprieve, they readily agreed. They set down the baby carriers and headed to their room for a much needed nap. Lucien sat up and carried Nellie to her room, gently placing her in her cradle. He went back to the living room to help Lanie with the other children, even changing their diapers when needed. He was determined to show Lanie what a good mate he would be.

Lanie was surprised at Lucien's 'domestic' side. Though changing diapers was obviously not his favorite thing to do, he did it without complaining. Lucien would keep changing diapers as long as Lanie kept rewarding him with a kiss each time he did so.

Mike and Devon were still asleep and the triplets had finally settled down to sleep in their cradles. Lanie went into the kitchen and Lucien made a quick phone call in the living room. Lucien ended his call and went to the kitchen, finding Lanie at the sink, washing dishes. He moved to stand behind her, began massaging her shoulders.

"Mmmm…," Lanie purred as she leaned her head back slightly to rest on his chest. Unable to resist her exposed neck, Lucien rubbed his stubble covered cheek against her neck and she gasped at the rough sensation. He nibbled and sucked on her neck and Lanie held onto the counter for support. Her legs felt strange, suddenly becoming weak. She was glad Lucien had wrapped his arms around her waist, keeping her from sinking to the floor.

Lanie began panting and her heart beat faster. Lucien slipped his hand down her hip and began pulling up her dress, all the way up to her waist. His hand found the waistband of her panty and he began tugging it down.

"Lucien, what are you doing?"

"Everyone is asleep, Lanie," he whispered in a husky voice as he nibbled on her neck. Lucien pressed his erection into her and she groaned. He held her hips and rubbed against her, then slipped one hand around to her belly, lowering it until his fingers were nestled between her legs. He rubbed his fingers along her seam and Lanie bit her lip as she pushed back into him. His fingers caressed her harder and she began writhing against him.

"Lucien," she moaned. He bit her neck gently, marking her again.

"Ohh!" she exclaimed when she felt his teeth close around the skin on her neck. Impatient, he again reached for the waistband of her panty and began tugging it down.

"Lucien, stop. We're in the *kitchen*!" she protested.

"I *need* to fuck you, Lanie. You've already made me wait too long."

"What are you talking about? We just met a few days ago!" Lucien was moving too fast. *Much* too fast!

"From the moment I saw you at Jack's, I wanted

you, Lanie. If you were a wolf, I would have carried you off and fucked you that same night."

"*What?*" Lanie stilled and her desire instantly vanished. *This is just about sex?* Foolishly, she had thought he wanted a relationship with her. But all he wanted was sex. Anger surfaced and she turned and pushed him away.

Lucien scented her anger and saw the fury on her face as she turned.

"Love, what's wrong?"

"Don't call me that!" She crossed her arms and asked, "So If I was a wolf, you'd have treated me differently?"

Unsure of where she was going with her question, Lucien nodded slowly.

"So just *how many wolves* have you…*bedded* right after meeting them?" she demanded angrily.

FUCK. "*None.* Honey, it's not like that. I just meant that…a female wolf would have understood my desire. A female wolf would *never* have run from me." Would she understand the compulsion wolf mates had towards each other? Lanie *was* human. *Could* she feel the same way about him?

Lanie was livid. *The only reason he had been nice to me, had 'dated' me was because I'm human? Not because he has feelings for me? What was I thinking? How could I have fallen for him? I'm so naïve. I should have known better than to fall for an Alpha. This will never work. We're just too different.*

Lucien was confused. Everything he said seemed to anger instead of soothe her. Perhaps he should treat her as a wolf, not a human?

"You're *mine*, Lanie," he asserted as he grasped her arms, pulling her closer. His wolf eyes flashing bright blue, he declared, "You belong to *me*, Lanie. I will *kill* any man that touches you."

Lanie's mouth dropped open in shock. "You're unbelievable! How *dare* you? *You don't own me!*" She pulled out of his grasp and moved away from him. "I'm *not* one of your wolves. You can't order me around! I'll see *whoever* I want, *whenever* I want. Now, *get out*!" She pointed in the direction of the front door. Lucien growled when he heard the front door open and scented Riley. Hearing voices, Riley walked into the kitchen and Lanie turned in surprise at his unexpected arrival.

"What are you doing here, Riley?"

"I came to check up on my kid sister and nieces. Mom said they were sick and in the hospital."

"Everyone's asleep, Riley. You can wait. I'm sure Devon will be up shortly," she said in a kind voice. Lucien growled a low warning at Riley. His wolf didn't like the way Lanie spoke to the other wolf, the one she had desired only days ago.

Hearing his growl, Lanie announced, "Lucien was just leaving."

Not wanting to cause problems with Ethan's pack, he decided to leave. As he drove back to Last Hope, Lucien decided he would talk to her the next day. She should have calmed down by then.

Later that evening, during dinner, Devon noticed that Lanie seemed unusually quiet. Had she gotten over her infatuation with Lucien? When Devon recalled the earlier message from her sister-in-law, a member of the Tarchannen pack, she was glad Lanie was no longer interested in Lucien.

After dinner was over and Lanie was helping her with the triplets, Devon shared some information about wolves and their curiosity about humans. If

Lanie had not already been heartbroken, she would have been after her chat with Devon.

Devon told Lanie that werewolves sometimes slept with humans. Devon warned her that they considered it something of a novelty. But they would never consider mating with one, as pack law wouldn't allow it. Werewolf birth rates were very low, which was why so many wolves showed up to the triplets' birth celebration. No one knew why their population had been declining. From an early age, wolves were taught to find their mate, in hopes of reproducing and increasing their dwindling population. As Alpha, Lucien had a *duty* to his pack to provide them with werewolf pups. Devon told Lanie that Lucien had returned home to choose a mate from the Tarchannen pack.

CHAPTER FIVE

Lucien drummed his fingers on his desk and tried to contain his anger. "You are thirty years old, Lucien. As Alpha of our pack, you need to take a mate, set an example for our younger wolves. Jordan of the Tarchannen pack has offered any of his single females to you as a mate. You must choose one of them," Richard, one of the pack elders stated.

"I don't want *any* of them," Lucien declared.

"They have traveled a long distance to see you, Lucien. The least you can do is meet them. It would be rude not to greet them," advised Stella, another elder.

"Fine. But I'm *not* mating with any of them."

"Lucien, these are beautiful young wolves. You cannot make such a decision without at least fucking them," David insisted.

"Enough!" Lucien slammed his hands down on the desk and stood, wolf eyes flashing angrily at the elders in front of him. "I'm not fucking *anyone* but Lanie. *Lanie is my mate*. My wolf will not have another." The elders gasped in shock.

"Lanie is the...the *human* you brought here?" George asked with contempt.

"*Careful*, George. That is *my mate* you are talking about," Lucien warned.

George lowered his eyes in submission. A former member of the Tarchannen pack, he disapproved of having a *human* mate. *Their offspring, IF they had any, would be mongrels, half breeds. They would be hideous freaks of nature that would bring shame to our pack. Something has to be done to prevent their alpha from mating with a* human.

"Why the hell is Jordan so interested in my finding a mate anyway?" Lucien asked the elders.

"Jordan wants an alliance with our pack. Our numbers are dwindling, Lucien. We need each other for protection, camaraderie. That is another reason you should choose a wolf. We need more pups. You owe it to your pack, to your kind, to mate with a wolf and provide pups."

"No one knows why our population is dwindling, but I will *not* give up my mate to satisfy this council. The subject of my mate is not up for further discussion." He paused and looked at each elder. They lowered their eyes in submission, acquiescing to his decision as their Alpha.

"As for an alliance with Tarchannen, I will have to think about it. Tarchannen are purists and old fashioned in their ways. I don't agree with their practice of assigning mates based on an Alpha's whims. If they have not found their true mate, couples should be allowed to choose their mate." Some of the elders nodded in agreement.

Lucien took a deep breath and continued, "I will meet these Tarchannen females then you will send them home tomorrow. I will contact Jordan once my decision is made."

Not wanting to scare the Tarchannen females, Lucien took several calming breaths. He went to Rae's and met the single Tarchannen females. He apologized sincerely for their trip and informed them that he recently found his mate. Several of the females seemed disappointed, upset that they lost the chance to become his Alpha Bitch. Lucien spent some time with them to be sociable. Someone suggested they pose for a few pictures. Lucien sat on a chair, surrounded by the Tarchannen females. Once the photos were taken, he excused himself and went home.

The next day Lucien showed up with a dozen white roses. "Whatever I said to offend you, my Love, I'm sorry. Please forgive me?" he asked. She would accept his apology and he would finally be able to fuck her.

Lanie's throat closed tightly and she was unable to answer him. She didn't want to be just a one night stand or a novelty lay. She knew she couldn't resist Lucien, wanted him too much. Enjoyed the way he made her body feel alive. If she continued seeing him, she would give in to her desire for him. He would break her heart and it wouldn't even mean anything to him. She meant nothing to him, now that he had chosen a mate. She wondered how many of those wolves he had slept with before making his decision. *Why was he here anyway? Shouldn't he be with his mate? Or was curiosity about sex with a human more important than his new mate?* Angry and hurt, Lanie closed the door, leaving him standing there, roses in hand.

Lucien could scent her pain, saw the sadness in her

eyes. Before he could explain, she closed the door firmly in his face. He banged on the door, rang the doorbell. After fifteen minutes, he finally decided to leave, growling in frustration. What had changed? He thought back to the time he had spent with her. He still didn't understand why she was avoiding him, but he vowed he would find out. There was only one way to do that….

Later that day….

"Do you really think that kidnapping her is the answer? She's going to be seriously pissed. Hell, she might even maim *me* for agreeing to this," Michael stated with a worried look.

"I've tried everything else and *still* she refuses me. This is the only way to satisfy my wolf. *She is mine. My mate*. I claim her before you and everyone else. She just refuses to accept it. Your sister is more stubborn than I am," Lucien said with a sigh.

"I swear to you, I will not force her into my bed. But I will force her to admit her feelings for me. I will keep her for two days, to convince her that she belongs with me. If she refuses me after that time, I will leave her alone. I only wanted you to be aware so that I don't inadvertently start a pack war. The last thing I need is a pissed off brother coming after me to protect his sister." Michael laughed.

"And who is going to protect *you* from *her*? You better know what you are doing, Lucien. It might cost you your balls. Literally."

"She is *everything* to me, Michael. I only wished she hadn't pushed me to do this. I do not wish to anger her. I am going to meet with your Alpha in the next hour, so he is aware of my plans. If you have any objections, state them now. I asked you to come here, to the forest, so we could converse in private. If you wish to fight me for your sister, you may do so without causing any issues between our packs. This is between two men. It is not a concern for either pack."

Michael studied him for a moment. "You are full blood and an Alpha. I am a changeling and have a low pack rank. Do you think this is a fair fight?"

"You would be fighting for your sister."

"And you would be fighting for *your mate. Nothing* could stop you. I have no objections as long as you agree not to force her to your bed. If you hurt her, nothing will stop me from coming after you. Do we understand each other?"

"We do, brother."

Armed with his future brother in law's blessing, as well as understanding from the Second Chances Alpha, Lucien began to implement his plan.

CHAPTER SIX

The following day, Lucien watched silently from the trees as her car pulled up and parked by the side of the road. Lanie got out and walked around, glancing around and seeing no one. She headed for the lake, as the note instructed her. As she neared the lake, he stepped out from behind the trees.

"Waiting for someone?" asked Lucien. Lanie froze. Slowly she turned around and saw Lucien standing behind her. Though she was still angry with him, some small part of her was elated to see him.

"You make time for Riley, but not for me," he said angrily. Shit, she thought. He was seriously pissed at her. Realization dawned. "You wrote the note, didn't you?"

"It was the only way to get you to see me." He advanced and Lanie turned and ran, glad she had decided to wear sneakers and jeans. She needed distance between them otherwise she might give in to her desire for him. She would despise herself for sleeping with him when he already chose *another* woman. Lucien swore and took off after her. She didn't get very far before she tripped and fell flat on her face.

"Lanie!" Lucien cried out in alarm. Within minutes he was by her side, pulling her up and checking her for injuries.

"Are you hurt?" More embarrassed than hurt, she shook her head. "No. I'm fine."

"Good," he said, as he tossed her over his shoulder and began walking towards the cabin. *What the hell?*

"Put me down this instant! Lucien, I mean it. Put me down RIGHT NOW!" Lanie shouted. She kicked her legs and pounded on his ass.

"You're right, Darling. I deserve a spanking. I've been *very* naughty," Lucien said with a chuckle.

"Are you enjoying this? Really?! Damn it! Put. Me. DOWN!" she yelled again. But she stopped hitting his ass, just in case he really did enjoy it. Why was he doing this? Shouldn't he be with his mate?

"Lucien, please, my head is starting to hurt." He stopped and immediately put her on her feet. She felt lightheaded as the blood from her head suddenly rushed back down into her body. She grabbed his shirt to steady herself. He quickly picked her up in his arms, cradling her and continued walking towards the cabin.

"I told you what would happen if you ran from me, Lanie. You chose this."

"You…you can't really mean…You're going to force me?" She asked him, shocked at his words.

"If I was going to rape you, Lanie, I would have ripped off your jeans, put you on your hands and knees and taken you like an animal until you screamed my name." Lanie gasped. *Why does the image of them in that position turn me on so much? What is* wrong *with me?* Lucien knew she was suddenly aroused.

"Does my mate want it rough?" he asked in a gruff voice.

"No!" she denied, shaking her head. *Did he just say* mate*?*

"I would never force you, Lanie. You will come willingly to my bed. And my wolf will pleasure you until you say you are mine. I won't take off my clothes until you beg me to, sweet heart. "

"Beg? Beg! Never. You must be out of your mind if you think—"

"Welcome to our Love Nest," he said as he set her down and closed the door. He locked it and walked past her to the table and picked up something.

"It's not fully charged yet, but you can still use it to call your brother."

"What is it?"

"A satellite phone. Your cell won't get reception out here."

"You're going to allow me to call him? Aren't you afraid of what he and the pack will do to you for kidnapping me?"

"He knows. So does the Alpha. They gave me their blessing."

"He WHAT?" Lanie stared at a grinning Lucien.

"He wouldn't!"

"Here's the deal: Give me two days to win your heart, Lanie. If, at the end of two days, you still refuse me, I will leave and you will never see me again."

"What?...Never?... I thought...but, but didn't you just say we were mates…." She was confused.

"We *are* mates, but if I can't convince you of this

in the next two days, then I don't deserve you."
"Deal?"
"Deal."

CHAPTER SEVEN

Lanie fantasized about the ways she was going to kill her brother when she saw him in two days. *I still can't believe he agreed to Lucien's crazy plan. Hell, I can't believe I agreed to it.* She didn't exactly have a choice, she reasoned.

Lucien had made a wonderful dinner then he disappeared. During dinner, he had kept the conversation light. They had talked about their respective childhoods, pack events, even the weather. Everything except being mates and what that meant as his status as Alpha. After dinner he had excused himself, leaving Lanie alone in the cabin.

Lanie paced around the small cabin, pretending not to notice the inviting king sized bed in the middle of the room. She surveyed the small cabin. Next to the large bed, along the east wall stood a dresser and a chest of drawers in solid pine. In front of the comfy bed was a lumpy couch. Two chairs were placed on either side of the couch, flanking the stone fireplace that rose from floor to ceiling. What looked suspiciously like an authentic bear rug lay in front of the fireplace. To the left of the inviting bed was a small table where they had dined, and beyond that a small kitchen. A small door beyond the table led to the bathroom. Her eyes wandered back to the large bed.

He'd been gone for about an hour and she was beginning to worry. A soft knock on the door drew her attention. She got up and let him in. A sweaty Lucien came in carrying an armload of firewood.

"I thought you would like a fire tonight. I'm sorry I didn't think of it sooner."

"That's very thoughtful of you," Lanie said quietly as Lucien stacked the firewood and began a fire. He looked up at her and smiled wickedly, "I'm going to take a shower. Care to join me?"

"No!" she said. "I don't even have any clothes here. You could have at least told me to pack a bag!" Lucien tensed.

"You would have packed an overnight bag for Riley?" he asked as he stood and crossed his arms over his chest.

"Lucien…." Even if she denied it, he wouldn't believe her, so she said nothing. He turned and went to the dresser next to the bed and pointed.

"Your things are in here."

Lanie went to the dresser and opened the first drawer. She pulled out a scrap of lace.

"What the hell is this and whose is it?" She glared at him angrily, waving the lacy negligee at him.

"It's yours. Everything here is yours. I bought everything myself yesterday… Is my mate jealous?"

"I…you better not be lying to me, Lucien. I. Don't. Share." Lanie ignored his smug face as she rifled through the drawers, trying to find something that wasn't translucent and would actually fit her. Lucien beamed. If she didn't care, she wouldn't be jealous. There was hope yet….

He watched as she shut the drawers in disgust. She stalked over to his dresser and pulled out a pair of boxers and a pajama top. Normally he slept nude, but he had promised her he would not undress unless she asked him to. He smiled as she went into the bathroom to take a shower. Seeing her in his clothes would be an even better aphrodisiac than the lingerie he had purchased.

Lanie sat on the couch, nervously waiting while Lucien finished his shower. *What was he going to try next? How am I going to stop him? Will I stop him? Even if they were mates, what about his pack?* She couldn't ignore his obligation to provide werewolf pups for his pack. She loved Lucien deeply. She shouldn't allow him to throw away his status as Alpha for her. Besides, the wolf population had been steadily declining and they needed more wolf pups. *It would be selfish of me to put my needs before his entire species. Maybe once he sleeps with me, he will get over his sex with humans obsession and he will be able to mate with a wolf. He will be able to move on, but will I?*

Lucien walked out of the bathroom and went directly to bed. He lay on top of the quilt, hands tucked behind his head. He was wearing only the pajama bottoms that matched her top. He looked so damn sexy laying there, waiting for her. "Coming to bed?" he asked sweetly.

"No, thanks. I think I'll sleep on this…couch." Lucien bit back a grin. He had specifically purchased that couch *because* it was uncomfortable.

"The bed is more comfortable. Good Night." He

turned on his right side and closed his eyes.

Good Night! He was going to sleep? Why wasn't he trying to seduce me? Had he changed his mind? This odd feeling was relief, not disappointment, she told herself. Lanie stayed on the lumpy couch until she was sure he was asleep. Then she quietly got up, climbed on the bed and lay down next to him. A few minutes later he turned and threw his arm over her waist. She held her breath. When he didn't move again, she let out her breath. Then his hand moved up to caress her left breast and nipple. She bit back a moan.

"You're not asleep, are you?"

"Nope. Didn't I say you would come to my bed willingly?" he said smugly.

"This doesn't count!" she protested, pushing weakly at his arm. He continued to caress her breast and nipple then moved to the other one.

"Do you want me to stop?"

"Yes." He stopped caressing her breast and moved over her. His mouth found her taut nipple and he began sucking it through her thin shirt.

"Oh," she moaned and placed her hands on his shoulders. She intended to push him away but for some reason, her hands held his head and pulled him closer to her. He released one nipple and began sucking on the other. She moaned again, and her womb began clenching. She knew she was getting wet and couldn't stop herself from moving under him. She felt empty and wanted, no needed…something.

"Do you want me to stop?" he asked innocently. He knew how aroused she was and hoped this time she wouldn't deny them.

"Yes?" she stated uncertainly, wondering what he would do next.

He smiled and rolled onto his side and stared into her eyes, caressing her face. Very slowly he began to unbutton her top. Before he got to the third button, she pushed his hand away and grasped the shirt in the middle. She pulled hard, ripping off buttons, exposing her breasts to him.

He didn't wait for further invitation. His mouth locked onto her nipple and he began sucking. She felt a tingle all the way down to her clit. She moaned and held him tightly to her. He moved to the other nipple and sucked even harder.

"Oh, God, Lucien, I never knew anything could feel so goooood! Please don't stop. Please…"

He continued sucking on her nipple, and his hand caressed her leg, her thigh. Finally he slipped it between her legs and began rubbing her clit.

"Oh, Lucien!"

He released her nipple, moved up and kissed her passionately. He rubbed harder then suddenly stopped. He sat up and pulled off her boxers. He was dying to taste her. He spread her legs and began licking her. He sucked on her clit and pushed his tongue inside her, as deep as it would go. He continued pushing his tongue in and out of her as he would his cock. He went back to sucking on her clit, and pushed his finger inside of her.

"Lucien?! Oh my GOD… that feels amazing!" He increased the pace of his finger sliding in and out of her.

"Tell me you're *mine*, Lanie. Say it!"

"Yes, Yes! I'm yours, Lucien, *only yours*. Please.…" He used his mouth and fingers and she screamed his name as she orgasmed over and over again. He smiled and moved to lie beside her. He kissed her again, tenderly.

"I love you, Lanie." Why she was shocked at his admission, she didn't really know. He had made it clear how much he wanted her. She felt something hard pressing on her thigh and glanced down at him. She stroked his erection through his pants.

"Can I see it?" she asked shyly.

"I'm all yours, Lanie. You can do whatever you want to me."

"Take off your pants," she demanded. He removed his pants and she stared at his erect cock. It was

"Beautiful. It really is." She touched him and was surprised.

"It's so hard, yet so soft at the same time!" She knew she sounded like a dork, but she had never seen or touched one before. She blushed, refusing to look at him.

"I'm glad you like it. Touch me, Lanie. Please?" His voice was thick with desire.

Lanie stroked him, from base to tip. She enjoyed touching, stroking him. He felt so good in her hand. She continued stroking him and was surprised when he suddenly tensed and his body jerked a few times. She felt wetness on her hand and thighs.

"I thought…I didn't know you would… I really wanted you inside of me," Lanie said quietly, not looking at him. Lucien kissed her and assured her he would be.

"That just took the edge off. Now I can make love to you slowly. I know it's your first time and now I can be gentle with you."

He kissed her and worked his way down to her clit. He licked, sucked and put his finger deep inside her. Before she knew it, she was coming again. This time, he spread her legs even more and entered her slowly. She cried out at the sudden pain and he stopped, kissing her neck and caressed her breasts. He nibbled on her neck and Lanie gasped when she felt a zip of lightning move across her belly. Lucien began moving, in and out slowly as he gazed into her eyes. Lanie felt her womb clenching in response to his intense gaze. Lucien caressed her cheek then ran his finger gently across her lip. He lowered his head and kissed her as he pumped his hips harder. Lanie felt his tongue moving against hers and her hands slid up his arms, caressing his shoulders and slipping through his hair. She pulled his head closer, demanding more of his mouth. Lucien continued to move his hips against hers and Lanie began moving her hips to his rhythm, pushing her hips against his. Amazing sensations flooded Lanie as Lucien's body pushed into hers. The pleasure-pain she felt across her belly intensified and she began moaning, "Ohhhh."

Lucien raised his head and held her gaze. He pumped his hips harder, driving deeper into her as he declared, "You're *mine*, Lanie. I'm the *only one* that will fuck you. *The only one*."

Lanie's body responded to his claim and she orgasmed again, her body clenching tightly around Lucien's cock. Lucien drove into her faster and faster until he suddenly tensed and spilled his seed inside of Lanie. He kissed her softly as he pulled out of her, noting her sated look.

They showered and he got rid of the bloody shirt that had been underneath her. She went back to bed and Lucien walked over to his jeans, hanging on the chair by the fireplace. He checked his pockets then began searching the floor around him. He reached under the couch and grabbed something, then walked back to the bed.

"We are mates, Lanie. You are mine and I am yours. *Forever.*"

"But I thought it was against pack law to mate with humans." Lucien laughed.

"I'm the Alpha, remember? My word IS law. I now declare it perfectly acceptable to mate with humans."

"Just because you change the law doesn't mean your pack will accept me. And I thought you needed to mate with a wolf so you could have children." She worried about his status as Alpha, his pack's acceptance of her.

"No one knows why some of us are childless. We are fated to be together, Lanie. Perhaps fate will be kind and we will have pups together. Regardless, I will not choose another female. *You* are the only one for me. *The only one.*" Lanie smiled at him and he continued, "If they want me to stay and be their Alpha, they will accept you. Otherwise, we will leave them and you and I will be our own pack."

"You can *do* that?" He shrugged.

"Why not? There are no laws that guide how big a pack can be. Some wolves are loners. They choose not to belong to any pack. I was one until a few years ago. The old Alpha became sick and they needed someone to lead. I was chosen, so I came back." He paused.

"Don't worry about it Lanie. I'm *not* giving you up and they can't make me. Remember, I'm the Alpha." Lucien sat on the bed next to her. "I went shopping with your brother yesterday. He helped me pick this out." He opened the box and showed her the diamond ring.

"Lucien, it's beautiful!" She took the box and pulled out the ring.

"I wanted to get you the biggest diamond they had, but your brother said this was more of your style. If you want a bigger diamond, I will get it for you."

"Big diamonds are tacky and I think they look fake anyway. This is perfect!"

"Put it on, Lanie. Show the world you belong to me and *only me*," he said in a husky voice.

"Aren't you going to ask? You are supposed to say, Will you marry me?"

"Yes! I thought you'd never ask!" Lucien replied seriously. She laughed while he placed the ring on her left hand. Only Lucien would trick her into proposing to him!

"We don't have a ceremony for mates, but I know how important a wedding is to you. We will be married as soon as possible."

"I love you, Lucien."

"I'm glad you finally admitted it." He pulled her into his arms and they fell asleep.

CHAPTER EIGHT

Lucien woke up and smiled at his mate. He kissed her forehead gently, working his way down to her nipples. He began sucking on her nipples while his hands moved between her legs. He rubbed her clit in slow circles and she began moaning in her sleep.

Lanie woke up in the middle of an orgasm. She felt Lucien's finger buried deep inside her, felt his mouth on her clit. Lanie's body convulsed as she orgasmed and she called his name again and again. He chuckled and rose up to look at her.

"Good Morning, Mate." She smiled and kissed him.

"It certainly is! Lucien, I think I'm too sore…."

"I know you are, Love. We have to wait a few days before we can have sex again. But there are other ways to please me…you have two hands… and a lovely mouth."

"Lucien!" She blushed and looked away from him. She couldn't believe he wanted her to.…

"I would love for you to take me into your mouth,

Lanie. To feel your lips around me. To have you lick me, suck me until I come inside you…Maybe one day you will. For now, I will be satisfied with just your hands."

He knew she was aroused by his words. He grinned. It was only a matter of time before his virgin mate decided to find out what it would feel like to take him into her mouth. Until then, he would wait patiently….

Lanie took the bottle of lotion that he offered and looked at him quizzically. He explained how she should use the lotion to lubricate him as she stroked him. Lanie blushed, pumped some lotion on her hand and lay beside him on his right side, head on his chest. She placed one leg over his right leg, so that it was between her thighs. She touched him gingerly. The lotion was cold and his body stiffened at the sensation. Slowly, she applied the lotion as she stroked him, from the tip to the base. She moved back up again, gliding smoothly thanks to the lotion. Shyly, she dipped her hand lower, caressed his sac, squeezed them gently then moved back up to his thick cock. She stroked him gently, tracing the vein that ran along the length of his rigid cock. She swirled her hand around the top, then moved it from side to side as she followed the ridge at the top of his cock. Her palm caressed his tip as she moved her mouth over his nipple. She sucked his nipple tightly, nipping and licking as she rubbed the thick head of his cock. She stroked him from base to tip as her hot mouth sucked one nipple then the other.

One hand was on her head and he massaged her scalp. The other stroked her bottom, squeezing gently, occasionally one finger slipped between her cheeks, gently touching the opening to her ass. She tensed, but he didn't press further and she relaxed, even began to enjoy the sensation of him touching her bottom so intimately. She varied her strokes, slow and fast, gentle and rough as she brought him closer and closer to completion. Lucien pulled her head up.

"Kiss me," he demanded. She complied, kissing him as she stroked him faster. Tongues dueled, hands stroked and massaged. Lucien tensed suddenly and she broke the kiss, watched him as he spurted all over her hand, arm, thighs and bed. She couldn't believe it, but she enjoyed watching him, was surprised at the amount of seed he released. She bit her lip and wondered what he would taste like.

Blushing at her lascivious thoughts, she got off the bed in search of a towel to clean up the mess he made on the bed. She washed her hands and arm, found a towel and returned to the bed, handing it to Lucien so he could clean up.

"Do you want to see my wolf, Lanie?" She nodded, curious about what he would look like.

Lucien concentrated and his body changed before her eyes. She heard a slight popping sound as his body reconfigured itself. His mouth extended and his head reshaped itself to form a wolf's head. His arms and legs shortened and fur sprung up everywhere. He even had a tail! She was shocked to see the large black wolf standing on their bed, staring at her with Lucien's beautiful blue eyes. It was the wolf from her dreams!

Her mind couldn't comprehend how her large mate could shrink and reconfigure into the body of a wolf, almost half his human size. It defied all logic and reason, broke laws of physics and biology, she was sure of it.

She shook her head, clearing her thoughts. Even as a wolf, her mate was beautiful. She held out her hand to him and he walked over and sniffed her fingers, licked her palm.

"Eewww! That's just gross!"

Lucien's eyes twinkled and he seemed amused at her reaction. He put his head under her hand and she understood, ran her fingers along his head and ears. She petted him like she would a dog, scratching him behind the ears and stroked his thick fur as he growled a low sound.

"Can you understand me?" Lucien nodded. Lanie smiled at him in surprise.

"Want to go for a run?" Lucien nodded and wagged his tail and she went to the door to let him out. He gently nipped her fingers before leaving. She stood at the door, watched him take off into a run and admired the way his wolf body flowed. Lanie kept her eyes on him until he disappeared into the trees. She closed the door, locked it and got dressed. She decided to make brunch, as she was sure he would be starving when he returned. She wondered if he hunted like a wolf. Would he eat a deer or some other animal while in wolf form? She had so many questions for him, couldn't wait until he returned.

They spent the next few days learning about and enjoying each other's minds and their bodies. It was the best week of her life, Lanie thought as she snuggled into bed, her mate's arm wrapped securely around her waist.

CHAPTER NINE

"You don't need to be so nervous. Remember, we are mates and *no one* can separate us."

Lanie still wasn't convinced that his pack would accept her. She was a human. She fiddled with her dress, suddenly wishing she had worn her comfort jeans as he had suggested. Wanting to look presentable to his pack, she had refused to wear her ratty old jeans.

He took her into Billy Rae's. She was surprised at the transformation. Some of the tables had been moved towards the back, to form a very long buffet table. Chairs were lined up in preparation of the pending meeting. It was packed. All of his pack members were here. She had the sudden urge to turn and run. He must have read her mind because Lucien turned suddenly and picked her up. The crowd parted as he carried her to the front of the bar.

When he reached the front of the bar, he stepped up onto the raised dance floor, turned and faced his pack, with Lanie still cradled in his arms. A hush fell over the nervous crowd, as they listened to their Alpha.

"This is Lanie, my mate."

"Lucien, put me down!" She whispered loudly. She was mortified!

Several pack members heard her and gasped in shock. She dared to command the Alpha? They watched silently to see what he would do.... Lucien chuckled and put her down, keeping an arm around her waist. She was too pissed at him to be nervous. She glared at him then turned to face the pack.

"Hi. I'm Elaine. You can call me Lanie," she said with a warm smile. The elders came up and introduced themselves. They were older wolves and acted as Lucien's advisors. She spoke with them for a few minutes then Lucien led her away to meet with his Soldiers.

Soldiers were strong wolves who physically protected the pack. If there was a threat, the Soldiers took care of it. Soldiers were loyal only to the Alpha. As his mate, they would die to protect her as well.

Next he introduced her to all of his mated pack members. They all held various jobs within Last Hope, running the grocery store, boutiques, salons, and garage. Some were teachers, nurses, even police officers. Lanie raised a brow.

"We have to look like any other town. If we didn't have a police force, humans might become suspicious," Lucien explained.

His mother was in poor health, so she was at home with Lucien's stepfather. He promised to take her there after the meeting. So far, everyone had been polite to her.

Lucien left her with his brother, Matt and his mate,

Shelly, while he went to get them drinks. She chatted amiably with her new in laws and glanced around, staring at the familiar looking young woman who stood nervously a few feet away.

"Anya?...It IS you!" Lanie excused herself and walked over to Anya, giving her a big hug. "I didn't recognize you with all that makeup. And your dress! You look beautiful!"

Anya beamed. The Alpha's mate remembered her? "I sewed it myself…well, I had a lot of help from Beth." She indicated the young lady standing behind her.

"You are very talented, Beth. I've been sewing for years and the only thing I can make is a pillowcase!" Beth beamed at the compliment, smiling shyly at the Alpha's mate. Anya's close group of friends had been nervous about meeting the Alpha's mate after hearing how fiercely she had defended Anya. They were afraid they might offend her and anger the Alpha. When they saw her smiling and chatting with Anya and Beth, their curiosity overcame their fear. Many young wolves came up to the small group and Anya proudly introduced the Alpha's mate to her pack mates. The atmosphere seemed more relaxed and friendly as they realized the Alpha's mate cared about them.

A few pack members watched her and grumbled. They were unhappy their Alpha had chosen a human instead of one of their daughters. They disapproved of the way she had ordered the Alpha. A woman should know her place! She threatened their way of life. Already her influence was being seen in the young she wolves. They were getting ideas that they could be something other than a place for a wolf to put his dick, whenever he wanted. They knew something had to be done. They planned to meet later and discuss their options.

Lucien finally succeeded in prying his mate away from his pack and took her outside. He pulled her into his arms and kissed her. She rubbed up against him as he nibbled on her neck.

"Lucien…." she said in a needy voice. He groaned. He knew it would be a mistake to touch her but he couldn't help it. He pulled away reluctantly.

"I'm sorry, Love. We have to go meet my parents. I will make sure it's a quick visit."

They walked a few blocks to his parents' house. He quickly introduced her to his mother and step father, Dale. His mother, Kathleen, seemed to adore Lanie. She was glad to see that her son was finally happy. True to his word, they didn't stay long. He took her back to his pickup and he drove home.

Lanie was excited about seeing Lucien's home for the first time. She glanced out the window of his pickup and the area began to seem familiar. When he stopped in front of the cottage she turned to him, a puzzled look on her face.

"Why are we at your parent's house? And how come they didn't move in yet? I thought we were going to your house?"

"I didn't buy it for them, Lanie. I bought it for us." She was shocked. That was almost two weeks ago. He had bought them *a house*?

Lucien picked her up and carried her over the threshold, locked the door and took her straight to their bedroom. He placed her gently on the bed and gruffly demanded that she get undressed. Clothes flew everywhere as they quickly undressed.

He lay next to her and kissed her roughly. His

hands went between her legs and found her already wet for him. He alternated between rubbing gently on her clit and pressing his finger deep inside of her, thrusting in and out. She moaned when he began sucking on her nipple. She held his head tightly to her chest, pushing more of her into his mouth. She found his erect cock and stroked him. She loved the feel of him in her hand, thick and hard. Suddenly he got up and rolled her onto her front.

"On your hands and knees, NOW!" he demanded in a deep voice.

She obeyed and was rewarded when he pushed into her from behind. She groaned as he entered her fully. When he withdrew, she almost begged him to enter her again. Before she could, he entered her again, harder and deeper this time, hitting her in just the right spot. He moved faster and faster until she cried out his name, clenching tightly around him. His body jerked three times as he emptied his seed inside her. He pulled out of her gently and they lay on the bed, exhausted.

"Welcome home, Lanie."

CHAPTER TEN

Lanie excitedly decorated their home and planned her upcoming wedding. She also decided to have a house warming party and invite the pack members to her home. Lucien explained how important it was for pack members to feel welcome in their home, as they would come to him for advice or help if they needed it.

She ordered food from Billy Rae's and Anya and her friends helped her decorate, hanging streamers and balloons everywhere. They arranged seating inside her home as well as outside. Lucien's pack contained thirty five members, all of whom would be coming to their home this evening. She showered and wore a pretty floral dress. Lucien insisted she wear a crotch less panty, but she blushed and refused, too embarrassed to walk around his entire pack in a crotch less panty. She pulled on her comfy white panty and Lucien sighed, disappointed.

Pack members arrived in droves. When everyone was gathered, Lucien and Lanie welcomed them to their home. He and all of the males decided to go for a run and they went outside, changed into wolf form and took off into the woods.

Lanie was left with all of the females and younger children. She looked forward to getting to know her female pack members. They ate and chatted about her home, discussed pack life in general. Lanie learned some interesting things, like not all adult couples were mates. Some had searched for years and never found their mates. Not wanting to be alone, they chose a 'spouse' and lived with them. They were not true mates, but they treated their 'spouse' as if they were a mate. That meant they were loyal and faithful to their spouse.

The women broke off into smaller groups, some of them taking the children outside to play. Lanie joined a group of women and they spoke frankly. She learned about some of the outdated practices the previous Alpha had set into place. Some of the women were unhappy because they were not allowed to work. Their only jobs were to provide for their mate, providing food, a good home and sex. They felt like whores. The ones who objected were primarily those who were not with their true mates.

What really bothered her was how young females were treated. The previous Alpha had decreed that once a female was sexually mature, if she had not found her mate, it was her duty to provide sexual services to any male who was interested. They weren't physically forced, but they didn't enjoy having to provide sex for any single male who was horny. Judging from Lucien's behavior, she was sure young men were horny all the time. The previous Alpha had essentially turned his young she wolves into prostitutes.

"Is Lucien aware of this?"

She would maim him if he had bedded a young woman who felt duty bound to sleep with him. They shook their heads in denial. He had never approached a young female for sex, nor had they complained about the situation to him. They were afraid he wouldn't change anything. After all, he was a male.

Lanie was beyond livid when Lucien returned from his run with the pack.

"Lanie? Love, what's wrong? Have they said something to offend you?"

Lucien glared at the women surrounding his mate. They all lowered their eyes in submission. Lanie stood quietly, took his hand and pulled him into their room. Lucien stared at her in shock when she explained what she had learned about the way young females were treated.

"This ends now, Lanie. I didn't know, honest!" Seeing the shock and anger on his face, she believed him. He kissed her and they walked out of their room and he addressed his pack members.

"I've heard some disturbing news and I want to clarify something. Apparently the previous Alpha had some ill conceived ideas about women. Females are not here for a male's sexual gratification. No female has a duty to provide sex for any male." He paused to let that sink in. He heard shocked gasps from both males and females.

"The penalty for forcing sex or coercing someone to provide sex is death. If you have any concerns or issues, I will be happy to discuss it with you. My mate is available to you as well. She is your Alpha Bitch and will protect you as I do." Lanie gasped and looked at him in shock. Lucien chuckled, "Sorry, Love, it's a title of honor."

Lanie glared at Lucien, but allowed him to pull her into his arms and kiss her until she forgot why she was upset with him. Having worked up an appetite from his run, Lucien left her and fixed himself a plate. He sat down in the living room and patted his lap. Lanie sat on his lap and she held his plate. They took turns feeding each other. Having eaten earlier, Lanie nibbled occasionally as Lucien fed her.

Lanie noticed a tall man, his handsome face lined with ugly scars, standing by the patio doors. He stood erect, feet apart, arms folded over his chest. He surveyed the crowd and appeared angry.

"Lucien, who is that man?" Lucien followed her gaze. "That's Kane, one of my best soldiers."

"Why does he look so angry?"

Lucien sighed, "I'm afraid Kane is lonely. He fought well against the Lost Souls pack in my bid for Alpha and was badly scarred. His face is nothing compared to the rest of his body. He is loyal and a good man, but women seem to fear him. I think he's jealous of the couples here. In his mind, they are flaunting what he doesn't think he will ever have."

"He looks intimidating with those scars and he radiates danger. Why doesn't he think he will find his mate?"

"He has searched and not found her yet. Besides, he fears his looks are...off putting."

"Are you kidding? He's handsome in his own way. The scars are kind of sexy if you ask me." Lucien growled and his arm tightened around her waist. She laughed and said quickly, "Not nearly as handsome as you are, of course!" Pacified, he nuzzled her neck.

"Perhaps his mate is human, like me. How will he ever find her, Lucien? Do you think he ever will?"

Lucien shrugged, "I was lucky to find you Lanie. IF your brother had never been attacked, IF he hadn't survived and IF Ethan hadn't brought him to Second Chances, he never would have met Devon and had pups. I would never have met you. Funny how things work out."

"Hmmm, that's a lot of 'IF's.' I'll be back later." She kissed him and stood, walked over to the table and filled a plate with all kinds of goodies. She picked up a fork and napkin then grabbed a cold beer. She walked over to Kane and stood in front of him. He was even taller than Lucien, so she craned her neck to look up at him.

"Hi, Kane. Want a beer?" She offered him the beer. Surprised at her offer and kind smile, he nodded and took the beer from her. He twisted off the cap and took a long swig. She offered him the plate as well. He was hungry but refused to walk over to the table, didn't want to walk past the mated couples or be near the single females who avoided him. It was just too painful.

"Thank you." He took the plate and she pointed to the vacant loveseat. He sat down and she sat right next to him.

"Mind if I keep you company?" He shook his head then glanced across the room at his Alpha, who was looking at them intently. Would the Alpha be upset that his mate was sitting with Kane? He didn't look angry at the moment, but he knew how quickly males could lose their tempers when it came to their mates. He was a strong solider, but he wouldn't stand a chance against a pissed off Alpha defending his mate.

Lanie followed Kane's gaze and winked at Lucien. He saw her wink and grinned, shook his head. She was up to something and he was intrigued. Lanie turned back to Kane.

"Don't worry about him. I told him I thought you were handsome." Kane nearly choked on his dinner. He looked at Lanie then back at Lucien, worry lining his scarred face. Lanie laughed, "I also told him he was far more handsome than you are, so he will let you live." Kane didn't seem relieved. "Why would you do that?"

"Are you kidding? You know how jealous mated males are."

"No, I meant, why would you tell him you thought *I* was handsome? I am badly scarred. Not just on my face."

"Because it's true. You are good looking. The scars don't detract from your looks. It makes you more appealing." She lowered her voice, "I know you long for a mate. I'm sure you will find her one day. Perhaps she's a human?"

Kane blinked. "I hadn't thought of that. Do you really think a human could accept me?" Female wolves didn't. Why would a human?

Lanie nodded. "I'm human and I think you're attractive. I'm sure your mate will as well." Kane thought about what she said. Perhaps he should give human females a chance. She sat with him as he finished his dinner. Lanie asked him lots of questions about his job as a soldier and he answered her, glad for the company. He could see why Lucien had fallen for her.

Lucien finished his meal, tossed his plate in the kitchen garbage and returned to the living room, to find his mate still engaged with Kane. Not wanting to interrupt, Lucien walked over, picked her up and sat down with her on his lap. He had been away from her for too long, missed her touch, her scent. He hadn't made love to her since earlier that morning and his desire was building. As soon as his pack left, he was going to fuck her. He hoped they left soon otherwise he would kick them out. He needed his mate, needed to be deep inside of her. His cock twitched and she wiggled on his lap, tormenting him.

Nicolai sat across the room from Kane, observed as the Alpha's mate approached him and offered him a beer. He watched as Kane smiled and sat down, speaking softly to Lanie. He was surprised that Lucien didn't interfere, as he was a very possessive wolf. Nicolai knew that if she was his mate, he wouldn't let any male near her. He was glad to see his old friend finally at ease with a woman. It was a shame that she was already taken, as she seemed to enjoy Kane's company. Nicolai didn't leave his spot until he saw Lucien walk over and pick up his mate, placed her on his lap. He grinned. He knew Lucien would be kicking them out soon so he could take his mate to bed. *He* would.

Nicolai nodded to another Soldier who moved to small groups, suggesting they wrap up the evening's festivities. Nicolai figured the Alpha's home would be cleared within a half hour. He walked over to Kane and Lanie, nodding to Lucien.

"Lanie, my Love, this is Nicolai. He's another of my soldiers." Lanie turned away from Kane and smiled at Nicolai. She extended her hand and he shook it.

"Please tell me you have a sister. I'm sure Kane is

dying to know." Lanie chuckled and shook her head, "Sorry, only a brother."

"So Nicolai, I really didn't have a chance to chat with many of the soldiers or any of the other males tonight. I did have a chance to speak with the females and learned a lot about pack life. Tell me, what do you think about wolves living together even though they are not mates?"

Nicolai thought for a moment before answering, "I don't think you should get rid of that practice, if that's what you're asking. Personally, I would prefer to find my mate. I think we all would. Especially now that we see how happy Lucien is with you. But for some of us….some of us searched but did not find our mates. Should we live alone? Or find some measure of happiness with another lonely soul?"

"Well said, Nicolai. I take it you are ready to settle down?"

"Yes. I long to find a woman who will adore me the way you do Lucien."

"Have you met all of the single wolves?" Nicolai shook his head, "I've been to a couple of the local packs on business, but none of their females is mine."

"Kane said the same thing. Perhaps we can help our lonely wolves. Maybe a gathering of some sort for all of our single wolves?"

"That's a great idea, Lanie. Will you organize it?" Lanie nodded, happy to be able to help her lonely wolves find their mates.

"I'm not much of an organizer when it comes to that sort of thing, but I'd be happy to help you in any way that I can," Nicolai offered. Lanie smiled and thanked him. Kane stayed silent. He didn't like the idea of being publicly rejected by every single female wolf.

Soon after, their home was empty as the last pack mate left. Lucien locked the door and went back to the living room in search of his mate. She was gone. He sniffed the air and headed to their bedroom. Not there either. He called out to her. She didn't answer. He searched all of the rooms again, starting with his office. Finding no sign of his mate, he growled in frustration. He sniffed the air and scented her arousal, followed his nose to their master bedroom closet. He opened the door suddenly and Lanie giggled when she saw his expression.

He reached in, picked her up and slung her over his shoulder. He carried her to their bed as she giggled delightedly. He tossed her on the bed and pulled open one of the drawers on her night stand. He pulled out two thigh high stockings and climbed onto the bed. He tied one stocking to each hand then tied the stocking to the bedpost on either side of the headboard.

"What are you doing?" Lanie tugged on the stockings, but they were too tight and she was bound.

"I'm going to punish you for that stunt. I wanted to fuck you the minute they left. You've made me wait, so I'm going to make you suffer the same torment."

"Lucien, untie me."

"Lucien?"

Lucien smiled wickedly as he stood by the bed, refusing to answer her. He stripped quickly and returned to the bed. He lifted her dress and was surprised to find her bare underneath. "What happened to your panties?"

"I took them off after they left." He growled,

"You should have waited for me on the couch. I would have taken you there."

He studied his mate, tied to his bed. He should have removed her dress before he tied her down. Now he couldn't suck on her nipples, touch the soft skin of her breasts. He smiled, realizing that would torment her. Lucien stretched out beside her and trailed his fingers along her inner thigh. He moved steadily upwards, caressing her belly, moving down the other side, caressing her thigh. Lanie wriggled, trying to get his fingers to touch her between her legs. He touched and caressed her everywhere but *there*.

He continued caressing her while he rubbed his face on her breasts, concentrating on where her nipples would be. Her bra felt tight as her nipples pebbled. A familiar ache began to form and she bit her lip. Finally, Lucien touched her clit. He rubbed it gently then slid his fingers lower, slipping it inside of her. She groaned as he filled her with is thick digit. He pushed deep inside of her and withdrew, repeating this motion several times. Finally, he withdrew his finger completely.

"Open your mouth," he demanded. Obediently, she opened her mouth, curious as to what he would do. He put the tip of his finger in her mouth.

"Suck," he commanded, and she closed her mouth around his finger, sucked on it, tasting herself! He pushed his finger a little deeper into her mouth and she continued sucking on it. She swirled her tongue around his finger and his eyes darkened. She saw it glow briefly and change into his wolf's eyes. He growled, a low sound, one she knew meant he was deeply aroused. She realized that he was fantasizing that the thick digit that filled her mouth was his cock.

And it made her even wetter to think of his cock in her mouth. She sucked harder and said, "Hhmmmm," and Lucien lost control. He moved swiftly over her and she spread her legs. He entered her, thrusting hard and deep.

Lanie wrapped her legs around him as he fucked her. He removed his finger from her mouth and she felt disappointed at the loss. He raised himself up, reached down between them and rubbed her clit as he pounded into her. "Oh, Lucien, don't stop!"

Over and over, Lucien pushed his cock deep into his mate. Her moans and groans egged him on. Faster and faster he moved until her body tensed and contracted around him. She groaned a deep throaty, "OOHHHH!" as she orgasmed and Lucien went over the edge, spilling his seed deep inside of her. He kissed her tenderly and withdrew. He untied her and she lay there recovering.

"I hope you learned your lesson."

"I certainly did. I think I'll have to do that more often…." Lucien groaned. He would never survive if his mate tormented him like that on a regular basis. She sat up and turned her back to him and he unzipped her dress. She undressed fully and stretched out next to him, placed her head on his chest and began caressing his nipple.

"Ready for round two?" Lucien chuckled and nodded, allowing his mate to satisfy herself with his body.

CHAPTER ELEVEN

Lanie was thrilled! Her wedding had been perfect. Her father walked her down the aisle in her beautiful white wedding dress. They exchanged wedding vows and she was now officially married to Lucien, her mate. They danced, dined, ate delicious cake and now were on their way home in a limousine.

As soon as the limousine's door closed behind them, Lucien kneeled in front of his new bride, put his hands under her dress and removed her already wet panties. He stuffed them into his pocket and unzipped his pants. He was aching for her. She licked her lips as he spread her legs, pushed her dress up, over her hips.

He rubbed his cock along her slit and she groaned. He slid into her tight, wet channel. Promising he would go slower later, he moved into her faster and faster, rubbing her clit with his thumb as he pumped into her hard. He angled his hips and drove into her deeper. She raised her hips to meet each thrust, desperate to drive him deeper inside of her. His cock hit a small bundle of nerves and she orgasmed. Stars exploded behind her eyes. She bit her lip to keep from screaming his name, not wanting the limo driver to drop the partition and see them. He released his seed into her and kissed her tenderly. When they got home, he undressed her carefully and as promised, made love to her slowly.

While most of the pack danced and celebrated the joining of the Alpha and his mate, a small group of men sat huddled in the corner of the reception hall. Judging from the angry lines on their faces and tense posture, they were not pleased. They had to get rid of the Alpha. None of them were strong enough to best him in a fight. They would have to discredit him. Make him seem like an unfit Alpha to the rest of the pack. A well dressed wolf smiled evilly and leaned forward, sharing his idea. The other men agreed to the plan and the mastermind made a phone call….

CHAPTER TWELVE

Six months later...

Lucien froze at the door. He scented another male and it made him angry. The scent is so familiar... Riley! He opened the door and called to Lanie. The house was too quiet. At once, he knew she wasn't there. She had left with Riley. He had known something was wrong. The last couple of weeks she had been acting strangely. She refused his touch, claiming her breasts were too sore and she had bad cramps.

His heart felt as if a vice was squeezing it and he wanted to kill Riley for taking his mate. He would kill Riley, slowly, in front of his mate. He warned her about what would happen if she ever allowed another to touch her. Soon she would see he meant every word.

He was about to storm out of the house, intent on killing Riley when a familiar scent caught his nose. He turned around and walked into the kitchen. He saw the meatloaf and mashed potatoes on top of the stove. She made him his favorite dinner on the night she left him? Confused, he walked into the dining room and saw the table was set for two. Between the two candles was a small rectangular box. He opened it and stared at it in surprise.

Lucien closed the box and ran out of the house, the box gripped tightly in his hand. He got into his truck and sped all the way back to Second Chances. Forty five minutes later, he burst into Jake's and yelled, "Riley!"

Jake's was full of Riley's pack. It was their weekly pack meeting. All conversation stopped as pack members turned to look at Lucien. Riley stood up beside his father.

"Where is she, Riley? I know you took my mate. If she has been harmed in any way, you will beg me for death." He threw the rectangular box at Riley.

"Not even God can save you if anything happens to our child." Stunned, Riley opened up the box and stared at the home pregnancy test. It was positive.

"I...I didn't know. I swear... I never would have...." Riley said as he fell back onto his chair. To harm a mate or put one in danger was to court death. To harm a pregnant mate, a very slow and painful death.

"Tell. Me. Where. She. IS!" bellowed Lucien.

"She hasn't been harmed, I swear. I never would have done it if they were planning to hurt her. I was supposed to make sure you knew I took her, so I left my scent there. Then I came here to wait for you to show up. He figured you would be so enraged, you'd attack me and my pack would stop you. I took Lanie to a cabin, not far from your home. I...I gave her a shot, just to make her sleep. According to the plan, once my pack got hold of you, I would deny everything and make them go to your house. Lanie should have been returned by now. She'd be asleep and they would think you'd lost your mind, or been stupid enough to start a pack war over your woman. Either way, he would have you stripped as Alpha and he would take over."

"Who betrayed me?" asked Lucien.

"Dale, your step-father and his three sons. Dale was going to make his oldest son Alpha. They were going to make me a soldier."

"You put our pack in danger, put a pregnant mate in danger for your own benefit? You disgust me, Riley. You will be dealt with in a most severe manner," stated a very angry Ethan, the Alpha of the Second Chances werewolf pack.

"To use a mate in an underhanded fight for Alpha status is beyond reprehensible. Lucien, I pledge my pack to you. We will support you until you deal with your traitors."

"Thank you, Ethan. Once the traitors have been dealt with, we will make it official. Our packs will become allies. Riley, how are they to know that I have attacked you?"

"I was supposed to call Dale once I knew our people were going to check on Lanie."

Lucien and Ethan discussed their options. Once the plan was finalized, Riley called Dale.

"That son of a bitch nearly killed me! It took ten pack mates to haul his ass off of me...I think they took him to the jail. He was seriously pissed off, man...ok. See you then." Riley hung up. Unable to look at Lucien, he hung his head in shame.

Lucien and three Second Chances werewolves

took one of their black SUV's back to Last Hope. Three other SUVs followed close behind.

Lucien was tense as the SUV pulled up to his home. He was out of the SUV before the driver stopped fully. He ran to the door and yanked it open. The light scent of gardenias filled his nose and he bolted in the direction of his bedroom. Lanie lay still on the bed, her chest rising and falling with each breath she took. His eyes filled with tears as he pulled his sleeping mate towards him. He held her tightly. Lanie stirred. "Lucien?...Riley…tricked me…."

"I know, honey. It's alright. You're home and you're safe with me. You're *both* safe." Lanie stared at him and tried to sit up.

"Both? How did you know?" Lucien laughed and kissed his mate.

"I saw the home pregnancy test. Hell of a way to tell me." Lucien smiled lovingly at his mate and placed his hand on her abdomen.

"Lanie, Love, I would like nothing better than to stay here and celebrate our good news, but I need to have Dr. Mallory make sure you and the baby are ok. You were given a tranquilizer. I also need to take care of those who dared risk your life and the life of our child." Lanie nodded, knowing her mate would not rest until he was certain they were safe.

"Hurry home."

Lucien left his mate with the doctor and the three pack mates who came with him. He took the SUV to the town hall, where his adult pack members were gathered. Outside the town hall, one of the three black SUVs pulled up beside him. Ethan, two pack members and Riley exited the vehicle. Lucien headed inside.

"I spoke to Ethan, Alpha of the Second Chances pack. He assured me that Lanie was safely sleeping in her home. Lucien is unhinged. He attacked Riley without just cause. He could have started a pack war. Luckily for us, Ethan is willing to let it go. But Lucien cannot stay as Alpha. He is unworthy. I nominate my oldest son, Robert, as Alpha of the Last Hope pack… Does anyone object?" Dale looked around, pleased with himself.

"I object," Lucien stated loudly. Dale visibly paled. Pack members looked at Lucien and whispered to each other.

"I just left my pregnant mate with Dr. Mallory. Apparently, she was kidnapped and given a tranquilizer by a Second Chances pack member, Riley." Lucien's statement was met with shocked silence.

"We are pleased to hear your mate is with child, Lucien. But why would this…Riley do such a thing?" asked an elder.

"And if Riley kidnapped her, who returned her to your home?" asked another pack member.

"Why not ask him yourself?" The crowed parted as Riley was pushed forward. His pack mates and Alpha followed.

"Dale and his three sons had me do it. They wanted to set up Lucien so you would strip him of Alpha status." His shocking announcement caused a loud uproar.

"Silence!" Lucien shouted. Everyone instantly obeyed.

"Dale and his three sons used my mate to take my position. That is the coward's way. If anyone wishes to challenge me, do so openly. Do so NOW!" Lucien turned around slowly and looked at each of his pack mates. They lowered their heads and eyes in submission.

"The penalty for traitors is Death," Lucien declared. He turned and walked away, allowing his pack to enforce his judgment. Screams were heard all through the night.

CHAPTER THIRTEEN

Satisfied that both she and his baby were fine, Lucien held his mate close. His hand absently caressed her abdomen, still amazed that they were going to be parents. He was overjoyed. He hoped this was the first of many pups they would have together. They fell asleep with his hand resting lightly on his mate's abdomen.

When Lucien awoke, the bed was empty. He heard the shower running and smiled wickedly. He walked into the master bath and watched his mate wash her hair through the transparent glass. He watched the water run over her head, down her back and over her generous ass. Blood rushed to his groin and his erection grew. Removing his boxers, he opened the door and stepped inside. Lanie gasped when his arms reached around to caress her breasts. He took some soap, lathered it up and began to wash her breasts. His hands moved over her breasts, down her stomach and one hand dipped between her legs. He washed her thoroughly and pressed up tight against her. His erect cock rubbed against her bottom and she moaned. She leaned forward slightly, placing one hand in front of her to brace herself, the other one on his hand that was between her legs.

He slipped a finger inside of her and withdrew it. He teased her clit, rubbing it roughly in small circles. He pushed his finger back inside of her and whispered, "Do you want me, Lanie?" Lanie nodded. "Then touch yourself for me." Lanie gasped, shook her head. He placed his hand over hers, took her finger and rubbed it against her clit. His other hand was on her breast. His fingers rolled her nipple, pulled on it roughly. Lanie's breathing increased. He moved her hand lower, forcing her to slip it inside of herself. She bent forward slightly and began to moan as he slipped her finger and his inside of her. Her hips rocked back and forth, rubbing against his hard cock, pushing their fingers deeper inside of her. Her legs began to tremble. He moved their fingers out then back in, deeper. She continued to rock her hips, grinding her ass against his cock.

"Please, Lucien. I need you inside me." He loved it when his mate begged for his cock. He would never deny her. He withdrew their fingers, turned her around gently and positioned them so her back was against the wall. She placed her hands around his neck when he lifted her. She used one hand to guide him inside of her. He pushed into her slowly, gently and she wrapped her legs around his waist. She held on as he began thrusting inside of her. Using his shoulders for leverage, she rolled her hips, pushing off the tile wall to meet each of his thrusts. Lucien kissed her mouth, placing light kisses on her cheek and neck. His mouth found a secret spot on her neck, sucked on it and her body exploded with pleasure. Unable to resist his mate's tight channel clenching tightly around him, Lucien's body tensed and jerked as he found his release. He kissed her again, withdrew then lowered her gently. She reached for the loofah and began washing her mate.

After showering they lay in bed together, her head resting on his chest. He absently ran his hand down her back.

"Lucien?"

"Hmmm?"

"We got pregnant very quickly. Some couples have been together for years and they are still childless. Do you think it's because we are mates or because I'm human?"

"What makes you say that?"

"Simple biology, Lucien. When species become isolated, after a while, their population can decline due to higher incidences of birth defects. Basically you have a stale gene pool. When new species are introduced and mating occurs, populations sometimes increase because of fresh new genes being introduced to the stale gene pool." Lucien chuckled. *Leave it to my mate to figure out our problem.* Good thing she's a science teacher, he thought as he kissed her gently.

"I think you're onto something, my Love. Perhaps it is both. I will strongly encourage my pack members to seek out their true mates. Human or wolf, it doesn't matter as long as they are mates."

Lanie sighed contentedly and hugged her mate a little closer. She couldn't believe how much her life had changed in the past year. She was aunt to three lovely girls who happened to be wolves, mate to a handsome, sexy Alpha and was pregnant with his child. She was excited about her future with her mate and baby.

Then the phone rang and all hell broke loose….

AUTHOR'S NOTE

I'm sure you are wondering why everything is so nice and peaceful with Lanie and Lucien then with one phone call out of the blue, all hell breaks loose. Because he's an Alpha and this is what happens sometimes. Other wolves' problems will intrude on his peaceful life with Lanie. Lucien's used to it and Lanie's going to learn very soon that she's not *just* Lucien's mate, she's an Alpha Bitch with responsibilities of her own. I've included a sample chapter of Unwanted Mate, Book 2. Keep reading!

Summary for Unwanted Mate
Soul Mates Book 2

Unwanted, despised by his own pack, Zane hopes that one day he will find love and acceptance from his mate. His hope is quickly shattered when he meets Jackie, his mate.

Jackie is shocked to discover that her mate is a member of the enemy pack *and* her brother's murderer. When her Alpha, Lucien, orders Jackie to spend time with Zane, Jackie is forced to deal with the mating instinct. Jackie must choose whether to forgive Zane or fight her wolf's growing compulsion to mate with him.

Will Zane ever find love and acceptance or is he destined to be alone?

Unwanted Mate challenges the traditional mindset by presenting both Zane's and Jackie's perspective as their story unfolds.

ABOUT THE AUTHOR

Diana Persaud is a self published author of erotica. She has written several erotic novellas and is currently working on a dozen more.

Diana has a degree in science from Stetson University. She gave up teaching to pursue her dream of being a writer of romance novels. The inspiration of her first erotic novella, *Lucien's Mate* came from her own experiences. Like Lanie, the central female character in *Lucien's Mate*, Diana also heard warning bells when she first met her husband. After a much longer pursuit, she finally agreed to be his mate.

Share your thoughts:
Diana would love to hear what you think of her first novella, *Lucien's Mate*. Please leave a review:
*On the website where you purchased this Book.
*On GoodReads, Shelfari or other Book Club posts
*Tweet about it
*Mention it on your Blog or website

Connect with Diana
www.facebook.com/diana.persaud.146
Blog http://dianapersaud1.wordpress.com/
Follow Diana on Twitter to get advanced tweets about Promotions and New Releases: @LuciensMate
Don't forget to check out her webpage dedicated to Lucien and his pack, dianapersaud.weebly.com.

Discover other titles by Diana Persaud

Soul Mates Series
Unwanted Mate (Book 2)
Lover's Delight (Book 3)
Stubborn Mate (Book 4)
Abandoned Mate (Book 5)

Wolf Secrets Series
Isabella's Dilemma (Book 1)

House of Aldinach
Samael (Book 1)

Contemporary Romance
Wait for Me

Printed in the USA
CPSIA information can be obtained
at www.ICGtesting.com
LVHW010606230424
778126LV00048B/459